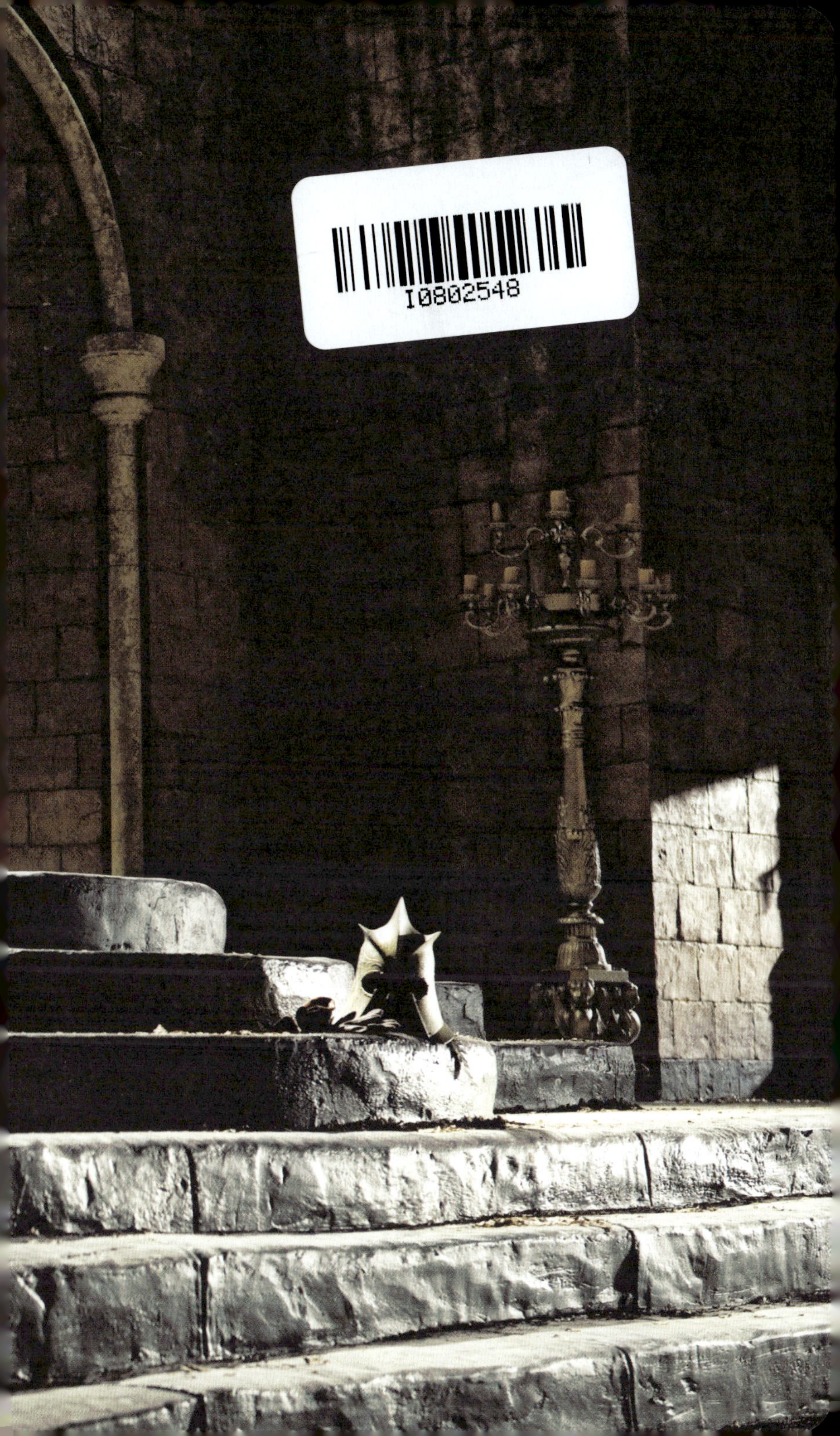

Property of:

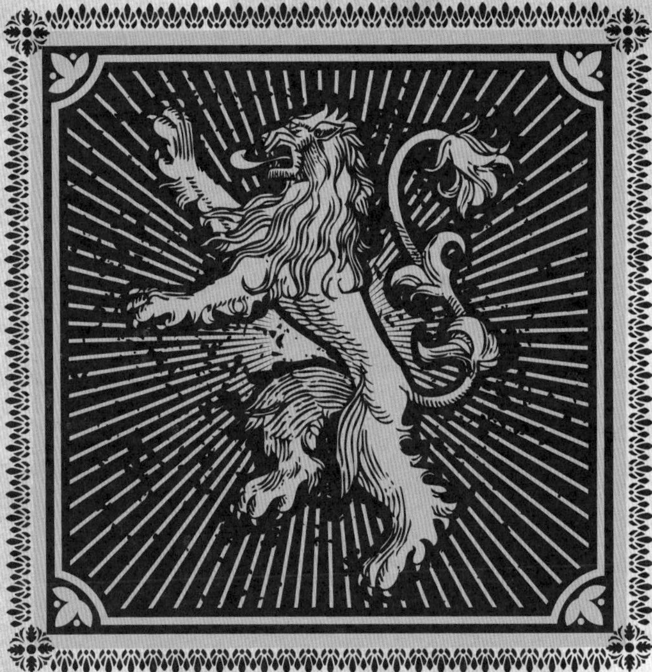

INSIGHTS

an imprint of

INSIGHT EDITIONS

San Rafael, California

www.insighteditions.com

HOME BOX OFFICE.

MANUFACTURED IN CHINA

10 9 8 7 6 5 4 3 2 1

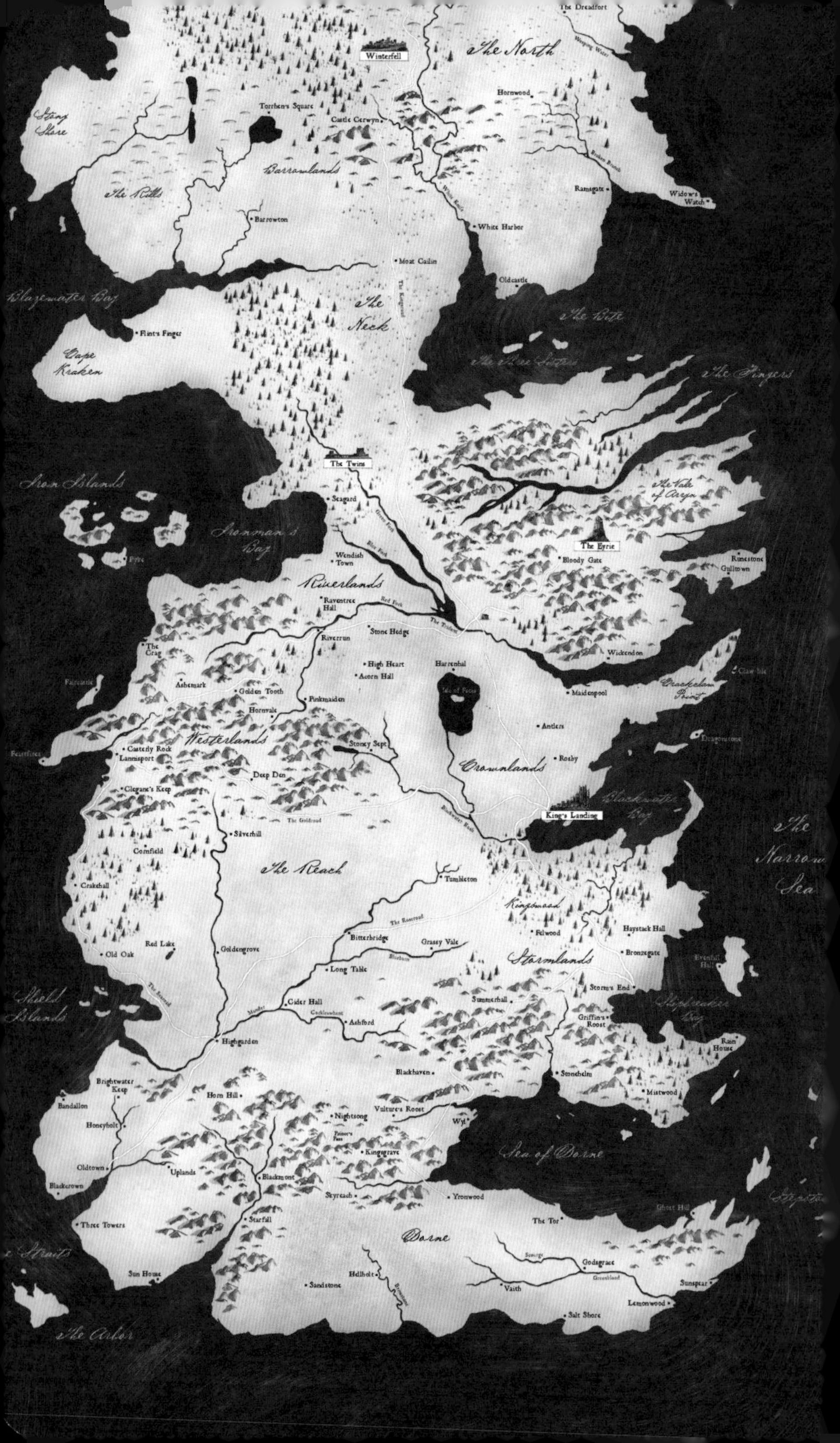
The Dreadfort
Winterfell
The North
Weeping Water
Hornwood
Torrhen's Square
Castle Cerwyn
Stony Shore
Barrowlands
The Rills
Broken Branch
Ramsgate
Widows Watch
White Knife
White Harbor
Barrowton
Moat Cailin
Oldcastle
Blazewater Bay
The Neck
The Kingsroad
The Bite
Flint's Finger
Cape Kraken
The Three Sisters
The Fingers
The Twins
Iron Islands
The Vale of Arryn
Seagard
Ironman's Bay
Pyke
The Eyrie
Bloody Gate
Wendish Town
Runestone
Gulltown
Riverlands
Raventree Hall
Red Fork
The Trident
Riverrun
Stone Hedge
The Crag
High Heart
Acorn Hall
Harrenhal
Isle of Faces
Wickendon
Claw Isle
Faircastle
Ashemark
Golden Tooth
Pinkmaiden
Maidenpool
Crackclaw Point
Hornvale
Antlers
Dragonstone
Westerlands
Stoney Sept
Casterly Rock
Lannisport
Feastfires
Crownlands
Rosby
Deep Den
Clegane's Keep
Blackwater Bay
King's Landing
Blackwater Rush
The Goldroad
The Narrow Sea
Silverhill
Cornfield
The Reach
Tumbleton
Crakehall
Kingswood
The Roseroad
Haystack Hall
Bitterbridge
Grassy Vale
Felwood
Red Lake
Goldengrove
Old Oak
Bronzegate
Blueburn
Stormlands
Evenfall Hall
Long Table
Storm's End
Shield Islands
Cider Hall
Mander
Cockleswhent
Summerhall
Shipbreaker Bay
Ashford
Griffin's Roost
Highgarden
Rain House
Blackhaven
Stonehelm
Brightwater Keep
Bandallon
Horn Hill
Mistwood
Nightsong
Vulture's Roost
Honeyholt
Wyl
Prince's Pass
Kingsgrave
Sea of Dorne
Oldtown
Uplands
Blackmont
Blackcrown
Skyreach
Yronwood
Ghost Hill
Three Towers
Starfall
The Tor
Dorne
Scourge
Godsgrace
Greenblood
Sun House
Hellholt
Brimstone
Sandstone
Vaith
Sunspear
Lemonwood
Salt Shore
The Arbor